What is phonics?

Phonics helps children learn to read and write by teaching them the letter sounds (known as phonemes), rather than the letter names, e.g. the sound that 'c' makes rather than its alphabetic name. They then learn how to blend the sounds: the process of saying the sounds in a word or 'sounding out' and then blending them together to make the word, for example c – a – t = cat. Once the phonemes and the skill of blending are learnt, children can tackle reading any phonetically decodable word they come across, even ones they don't know, with confidence and success.

However, there are of course many words in the English language that aren't phonetically decodable, e.g. if a child gets stuck on 'the' it doesn't help if they sound it out and blend it. We call these 'tricky words' and they are just taught as words that are so 'tricky' that children have to learn to recognise them by sight.

How do phonic readers work?

Phonic reading books are written especially for children who are beginning to learn phonics at nursery or school, and support any programme being used by providing plenty of practice as children develop the skills of decoding and blending. By targeting specific phonemes and tricky words, increasing in difficulty, they ensure systematic progression with reading.

Because phonic readers are primarily decodable – aside from the target tricky words which need to be learnt, children should be able to read the books with real assurance and accomplishment.

Big Cat phonic readers:
We Are Not Fond of Rat!

In Big Cat phonic readers the specific phonemes and tricky words being focussed on are highlighted here in these notes, so that you can be clear about what your child's learning and what they need to practise.

While reading at home together, there are all sorts of fun additional games you can play to help your child practise those phonemes and tricky words, which can be a nice way to familiarise yourselves with them before reading, or remind you of them after you've finished. In *We Are Not Fond of Rat!*, for example:

- the focus phonemes are qu (quack), th (them), ch (chat). Why not write them down and encourage your child to practise saying the sounds as you point to them in a random order. This is called 'Speed Sounds' and as you get faster and faster with your pointing, it encourages your child to say them as quickly as possible. You can try reversing the roles, so that you have a practice too!

- the tricky words are 'we', 'are', 'of', 'I', 'all', 'to', 'like', 'said', 'they', 'see' and 'was'. You can play 'Hide and Seek' by asking your child to close their eyes and count to 10, while you write each word on a piece of paper, hiding them somewhere in the room you're in or the garden for your child to find. As they find each one, they should try reading and spelling the word out.

Reading together

- Why not start by looking at the front cover of *We Are Not Fond of Rat!* and talking about what you can see.

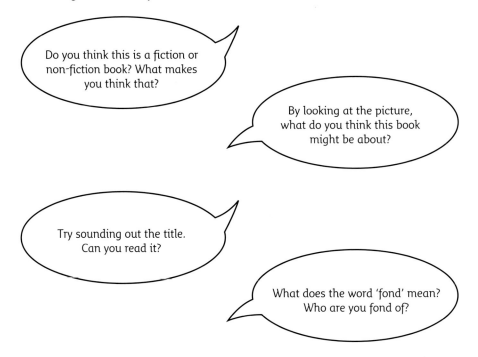

Do you think this is a fiction or non-fiction book? What makes you think that?

By looking at the picture, what do you think this book might be about?

Try sounding out the title. Can you read it?

What does the word 'fond' mean? Who are you fond of?

- Enjoy reading *We Are Not Fond of Rat!* together, noticing the focus phonemes (qu, th, ch) and tricky words (we, are, of, I, all, to, like, said, they, see, was). It's useful to point to each word as your child reads, and encouraging to give them lots of praise as they go.

- If your child gets stuck on a word, and it's phonetically decodable, encourage them to sound it out. You can practise blending by saying the sounds aloud a few times, getting quicker and quicker. If they still can't read it, tell them the word and move on.

Talking about the book

- Use the story map on pp18–19 to talk about the story together.

- Practise the focus phonemes from *We Are Not Fond of Rat!* by asking your child to tell you which sound, for example, the word 'quack' begins with, or how they'd sound out, for example, 'chat'.

We Are Not Fond of Rat!

Written and illustrated by
Emma Chichester Clark

Collins

Dog is fond of Duck.
Cat is fond of Bat.

I am fond of all of them,
but we are not fond of Rat!

Dog will quack to Duck.
Cat will buzz at Bat.

I will sing to all of them,
but we will not chat to Rat!

Dog and Duck cook pie.
Cat grills yam with Bat.

I bring a dish of mash and fish,
but we will not feed Rat!

Dog is mad with Duck.
Cat is biffing Bat.

I feel like bashing all of them,
but we will not bash Rat!

Dog is hitting Duck.
I think Cat bit Bat.

I said, "STOP!" but they just
went on, then I *see* Bat kiss Rat!

Dog and Duck and Cat
see that Bat is sweet to Rat.

"I wish I was not sad,"
Rat wept.
So all of us kiss Rat.

A story plan

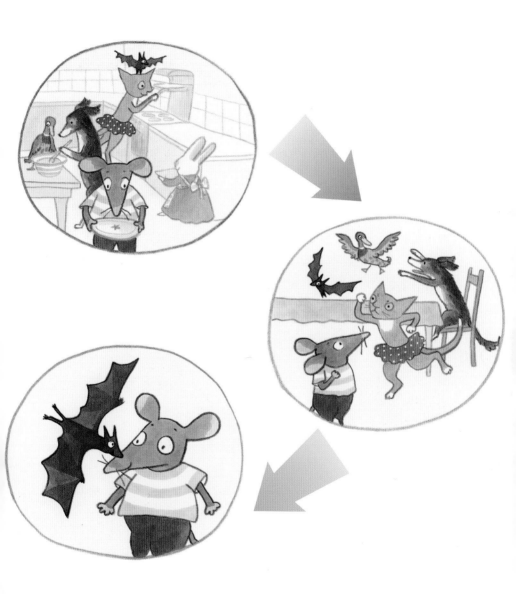

Getting creative

- Have some fun with your child by playing a running game, where they run, hop or jump towards different focus phonemes written on pieces of paper and stuck around the room. For example they could run to the 'qu' phoneme, hop to the 'th' phoneme or jump to the sound at the beginning of 'chat'.

- To practise the tricky words, why not play 'Fast Words', where you write all the tricky words down on a piece of paper and point to each one for your child to read, getting faster and faster!

- If your child's enjoyed reading *We Are Not Fond of Rat!* they could make a card for Rat from the other animals, which they could decorate.

- They might also write a message inside the card to cheer Rat up when he feels sad.

Other books at Level 1:

Fiction	Non-fiction
Sam and the N... (Giuditta Gaviraghi)	Got It! (Charlotte Guillain, Lucy Hamlin-Roberts)
Ant and Snail (Paul Shipton, Jon Stuart)	Pet Cat, Big Cat (Alison Hawes)
We Are Not Fond of Rat! (Emma Chichester Clark)	Pond Food (John Townsend, Pamela Anzolotti)

Collins Big Cat
Reading Lions

Published by Collins
An imprint of HarperCollins*Publishers*
1 London Bridge Street
London
SE1 9GF

Author and illustrator: Emma Chichester Clark

British Library Cataloguing in Publication Data
A Catalogue record for this publication is available from the British Library.

Designer: Rachel Hamdi/Holly Fulbrook
Parent notes authors: Sue Reed and Liz Webster

Printed and bound by RR Donnelley APS

www.collins.co.uk/parents